Before and Now

by Alma Flor Ada
illustrated by CD Hullinger

Harcourt

Orlando   Boston   Dallas   Chicago   San Diego

Visit *The Learning Site!*

www.harcourtschool.com

W9-AKV-686

Before, I walked with my mother to school.

Now I ride a yellow
bus to school.

Before, I carried my books in my hands.

4

Now I carry my books
in a red backpack.

Before, I wore a uniform to school.

Now I can wear blue jeans and a pink shirt to school.

Before, I went home
for lunch.

Now I eat lunch in the
purple school cafeteria.

Before, I played outside
in the green grass.

Now I play inside with an orange ball.

Before, I liked to play soccer.

Now I like to play basketball.

Before, my best friend
was Maria.